MW01043159

For Grandma.

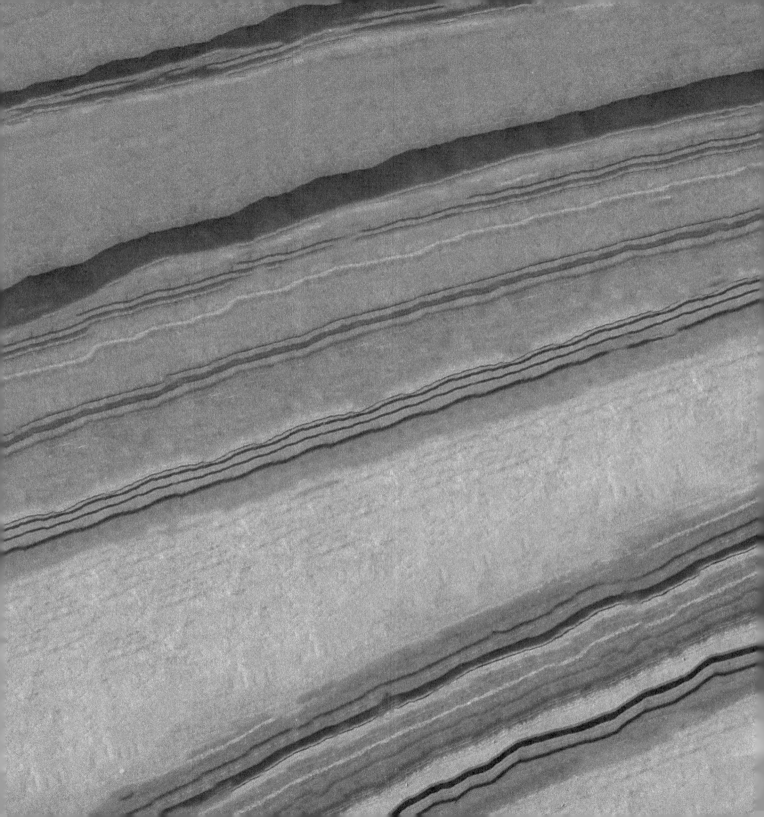

Way up north in the woods of Wisconsin,
time nearly stops, or at least it seems to on the
longest and coldest of nights.

When I walk the empty field back home from an evening of play, I hear the crunch of the cold snow against hard ice. That's the only sound between me and the quiet of the moon as it follows me home.

By tomorrow morning, a fresh
snowfall will fill in the sunken
steps which I stamp into the
ground with each boot.

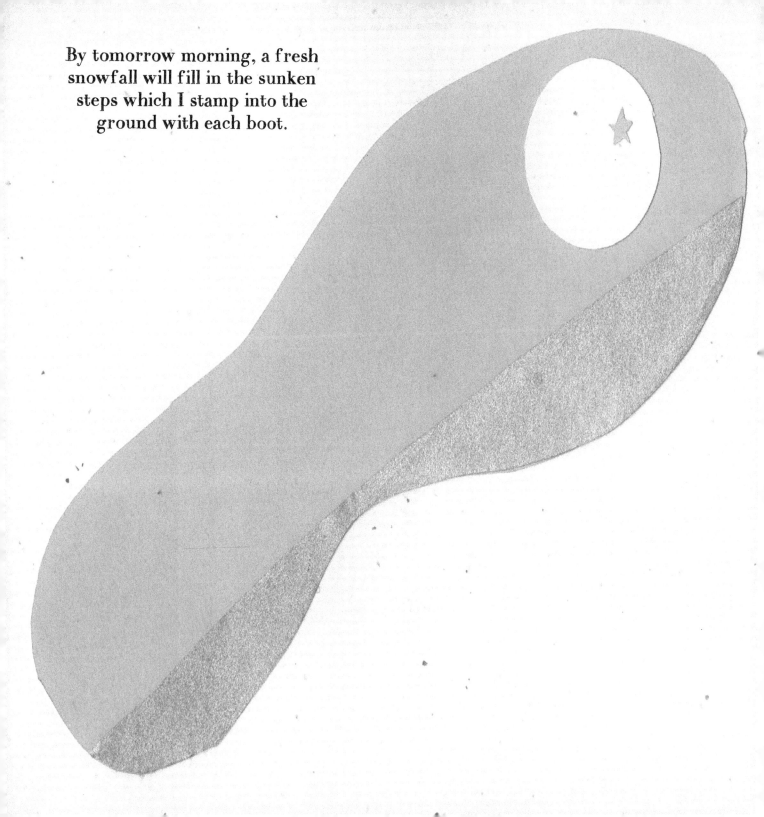

Every step my legs take, they do so at
winter's pace — each stride slower in
the cold, deep snow.

Winter is long, and spring is so far away that it seems real only to my imagination. I see the buds on Mom's bushes once again, just as they were so long ago, and I hear the faint melody of birds greeting each sunrise we woke up to.

The solitude of winter leaves the mind and spirit to long for the return of life and the colors of spring. But winter is the perfect time to reflect on the simpler things we overlook in the noise of everyday life.

I watch a snowshoe hare catapult through a snowdrift like a child catching snowflakes. When the snow gets really deep, I borrow Dad's snowshoes to glide through these banks with ease just like the little snowshoe hare.

When I get home, I look through a window frosted by the cold. I rub a spot of ice off and find a lone fox resting next to a stump Dad uses to chop wood in the fall.

I wonder, what's the fox thinking about?

She just sits there stealing time like the picture on an old glass negative: black and white, but beautiful.

With the warmth of my breath, a small view opens up. I watch from Grandpa's oak chair while my socks and mittens dry next to our stove and the smell of wood crackling in the fire fills our country home.

Outside it's a whitewash of winter until a snowy owl appears in flight to chase a barn vole behind our corn silo. I feel sorry for the little vole. He is easy to spot since the snow has covered the browns of autumn.

Our harvest is preserved in the jars Mom canned last Labor Day, and Dad has the freezer full of meat. We have plenty of food, but what do these animals eat when their environment is covered in a blanket of snow?

Over by the old pigpen, I count the points on a
big whitetail buck that's snacking on corncobs
left standing after the harvest. I'm sure
whatever he doesn't get will be breakfast for
the squirrels tomorrow morning.

The world is vast, and you feel its greatness up here in our little cabin watching everything from this little opening on our little frosty window. The silence of my surroundings is loud with life, yet it calms me to watch so comfortably from Grandpa's chair.

Seeing the animals brings me joy, and I go to bed relaxed and warm from the comforts of my quilt. I lie under the covers wondering about the animals outside. Which ones are getting ready to sleep like me? Which ones are outside, still awake and looking around? My thoughts are the lullaby that puts me to sleep.

In the morning, I eat my breakfast, a warm stack of silver dollar pancakes with butter and syrup running down the sides.

When I'm done, I put on my boots, mittens, jacket, and hat.
Then I go out the front door to play.

My tracks from last night have been wiped away
like an Etch A Sketch turned upside down. But
what was left is quite the surprise.

They were tracks, but whose tracks if they weren't mine? They weren't dog tracks, and they were much too big to be deer tracks.

I decided to follow them for a distance. They took me through a patch of red dogwood brush and into the forest behind our home.

For each footprint I
followed, I left my very
own right next to it until
I couldn't go any further.
I stopped at the edge of
our pond to marvel over
something big.

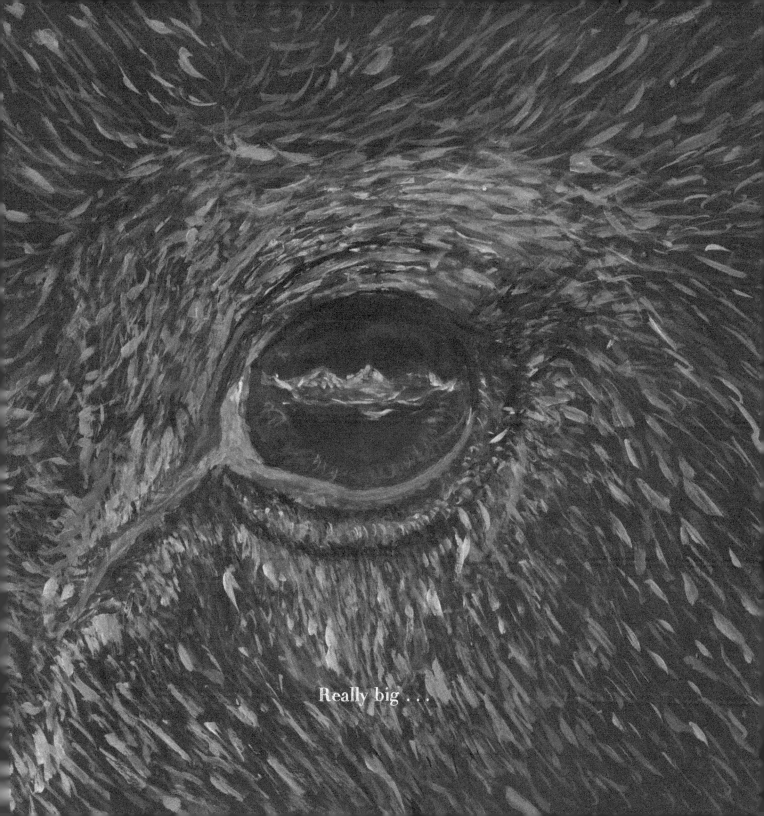

Really big . . . .

There, plopped firmly in the pond,
was a moose munching away on
cattails that were poking out of the
water like hot dogs on a stem.

It was amazing! I stood still and
watched her until it was time to return
winter's solitude to my guest.

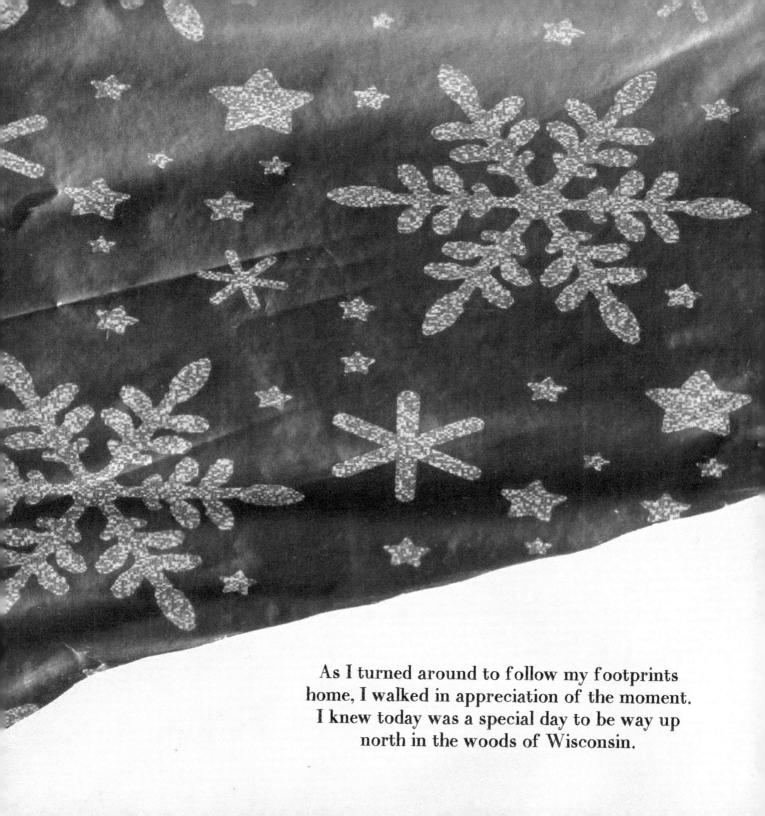

As I turned around to follow my footprints
home, I walked in appreciation of the moment.
I knew today was a special day to be way up
north in the woods of Wisconsin.

Winter Solitude
Copyright © 2022 by Jeff Lang
Written by Jeff Lang
Illustrated by Jade Lang
ISBN 9781645384496

All Rights Reserved. Written permission must be secured from the publisher
to use or reproduce any part of this book, except for brief quotations in
critical reviews or articles.

For information, please contact:
shannon@orangehatpublishing.com

Orange Hat Publishing
www.orangehatpublishing.com
Waukesha, WI

CPSIA information can be obtained
at www.ICGtesting.com
Printed in the USA
JSHW022251181022
31792JS00002B/86